Yasmin and Dad went to the bank.

Next, they went shopping.

Yasmin held the shopping list.

Yasmin and Dad went to a big shop. They got in the lift.

A man got in with them.

I like this pink belt.
Belts

I like this golf ball.

milk
This is the best lamp.

That cost a lot!

Yasmin and Dad got back in the lift.

The man got in with them.

Yasmin and Dad went back home.

A vest!

Milk!
milk

A pump!

That's odd!